Amelia Otter's
Mischief in the Water

By Luke McLelan

Illustrated by Nate Bañuelos

Amelia Otter's Mischief In The Water

ISBN: 979-8-9900900-1-9

Cover by Nate Bañuelos

Illustrations by Nate Bañuelos

This Book Belongs To

_____

As surfers who have spent countless hours in the ocean of the Monterey Bay, we'd like to thank the Monterey Bay Aquarium and Long Marine Lab for everything they have done for education and ocean conservation.

-Luke and Nate

Amelia Otter was a curious and playful otter who was born in the Monterey Bay Aquarium.

She spent most of her days
learning how to swim,

hunting
urchins,

and taking naps on her mother's tummy.

One day, she was swimming around her tank looking for something fun to play with, when she discovered a new toy.

This was the greatest toy in the world!

She could climb on it, sleep on it,
and even chew on it.

When Amelia was grown and strong enough
to survive on her own, she was released
into the waters of the Monterey Bay.

For two years, she had a great life swimming, diving, eating urchins, and meeting other otters.

As much as she loved living in
the Monterey Bay, she felt that
something was missing from her life...

but what could it be?

One day, as Amelia was exploring
new areas, she found a magical place
called Santa Cruz.

As she was admiring her new home, she discovered the one thing that was missing from her life...

A SURFBOARD

She had to have one of her own!

... but it's hard to buy a surfboard
when you're an otter.

Maybe the other surfers wouldn't
mind sharing with her?

At first, everyone was a little nervous
about Amelia borrowing their boards,

but after a while the surfers
accepted her as one of their own.

She really loved surfboards!

She loved the
way they felt,

the way
they floated,

and occasionally, the way they tasted.

One sunny afternoon, Amelia Otter was swimming around looking for a board to borrow, when she came across a man who did not want to share with her.

The man scolded Amelia and told her that otters don't belong on surfboards!

The man angrily drove home!

He could not believe an otter
would dare to take his surfboard.

The very next day the man called everyone he knew, including the mayor and the newspaper.

He explained to them how
he was harassed by Amelia Otter.

He told them all how otters
should not be allowed to surf.

If they didn't deal with it soon, otters
everywhere would be stealing boards.

The decision was made;
Amelia Otter's mischief must be stopped.

WANTED

ALIVE

REWARD $500

For board hoarding and wave
hogging. Do NOT approach.
Call authorities immediately.

SHE HAD TO GO!

At first they tried to swim up to
Amelia and capture her with a net,

but she always stayed
just out of reach.

Next, they tried to catch her with a boat,

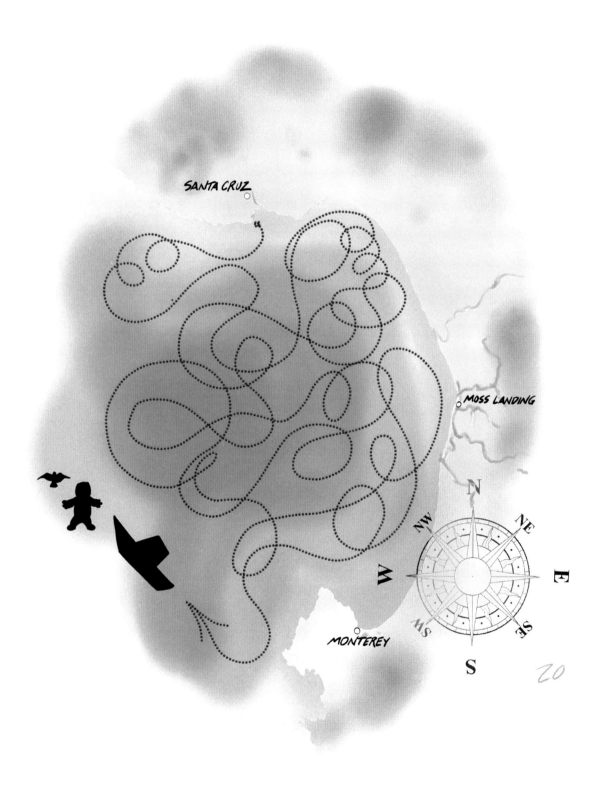

but she was too fast for them.

They even tried to lure her into the
boat by giving her HER OWN board,

but she was too smart to fall for that.

After many failed attempts, they
realized that Amelia
Otter could not
be caught.

Everyone agreed that she deserved to be surfing
the waters of Santa Cruz more than anyone else.

Eventually, the man accepted that
otters should be allowed to surf.

He even learned to share his
board and waves with Amelia Otter.

She now spends her days swimming, diving
for urchins, and, of course, surfing the
beautiful waves of Santa Cruz.

She is a true friend to everyone
and a local legend.

... Or is it?

Made in the USA
Las Vegas, NV
20 December 2024

14830720R00021